Young Learner's

Rumpelstiltskin

Once there was a poor Miller whose greatest treasure was his beautiful daughter. She had long, golden hair, eyes as blue as the deepest sea, and a warm, gentle smile.

One day the Miller, hoping to win the King's favour, boasted that his daughter could spin straw into gold.

The King loved gold more than anything else in the world. Everything in his castle was made of gold—the dishes, the tables, the royal flags, the swords, and even the horses' saddles.

Upon learning that the Miller's daughter could turn straw into gold, the King demanded to see her at once. "We must find out if this story is true," he said to the Miller. "Bring your daughter to my castle and we'll test her spinning skills."

When the Miller's daughter arrived at the castle, the King led her into a room filled with bundles of straw and a large spinning wheel, "You have to spin this straw into gold till dawn," he said. "If there is any straw left when the sun rises, you will die."

As the King locked the door behind him, the Miller's daughter began to weep. She had no idea how to turn straw into gold till dawn. Her father had made up the whole story.

Suddenly, a tiny man crawled under the door. He was the strangest creature the girl had ever seen. He was no taller than a chair. His beard was scraggly, his cap was tattered, and his face was as wrinkled as an old raisin.

"Why do you cry, fair maiden?" asked the dwarf in a screechy voice.

"Oh," sobbed the Miller's daughter. "I will die unless I find a way to spin all this straw into gold."

"May be I can help you," said the little man, "What will you give me if I spin the gold for you?"

"I will gladly give you my necklace," replied the girl.

The dwarf wrapped the necklace around his tiny neck and sat down at the spinning wheel. In just a few minutes, the room was glowing with gold.

The next morning, the King was so pleased with the piles of gold that he put the Miller's daughter in another bigger room.

"Cast your magic again," demanded the King, "Or you will die at sunrise."

Once again, the Miller's daughter did not know what to do. She began to cry.

As if by magic, the little dwarf again appeared. "If I help you again, what will you pay me?" he asked.

"Please take my ring," responded the girl.

The little man whirled and twirled the spinning wheel. Soon the large stacks of straw turned into glittering strands of gold.

The next day, the King was thrilled to see so much gold. But his greed was still not satisfied.

"I will give you one last test," he said to the Miller's daughter. "If you can spin all the straw in the stable into gold, I will make you my wife. But if the straw is there in the morning, you will die."

The Miller's daughter was terrified. She knew the stable was filled to the ceiling with straw.

Just then, the little man jumped over the stable door. "I will save your life last time," he said to her. "But you must reward me."'

"I have nothing left to give you," cried the Miller's daughter in despair.

"Promise me that you will give me your first born child," demanded the dwarf, "and I'll spin all this straw into gold before sunrise."

The Miller's daughter reluctantly agreed to give the tiny man what he wanted. She had no other choice.

The next morning the stable was sparkling in the sunlight. Gold hung from everything. There were even ribbons of gold in the horses' tails.

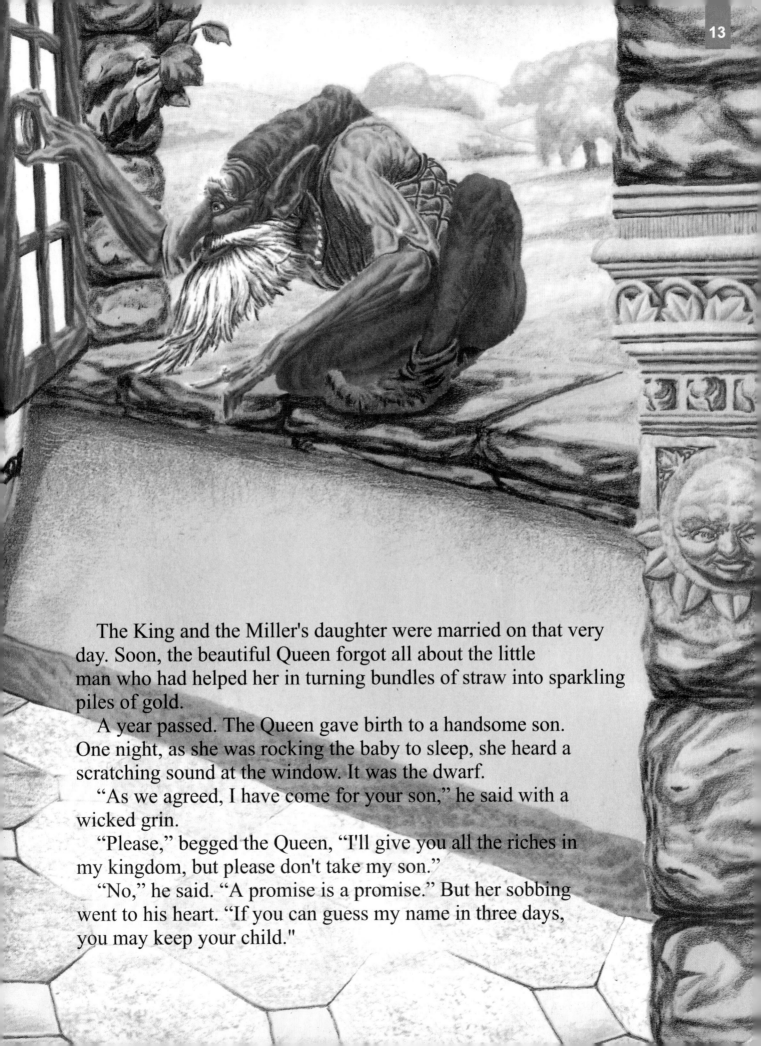

The King and the Miller's daughter were married on that very day. Soon, the beautiful Queen forgot all about the little man who had helped her in turning bundles of straw into sparkling piles of gold.

A year passed. The Queen gave birth to a handsome son. One night, as she was rocking the baby to sleep, she heard a scratching sound at the window. It was the dwarf.

"As we agreed, I have come for your son," he said with a wicked grin.

"Please," begged the Queen, "I'll give you all the riches in my kingdom, but please don't take my son."

"No," he said. "A promise is a promise." But her sobbing went to his heart. "If you can guess my name in three days, you may keep your child."

The next day the Queen guessed every name she could think of. "No, no, no," answered the little man every time.

The second day the Queen sent messengers to every corner of the country to find more names. She tried them all, but the dwarf just laughed and shook his head. The Queen began to despair.

Suddenly, on the morning of the third day, one of the messengers galloped to the castle. "Late last night I saw something very strange," he told the Queen. "On the top of a hill, next to a straw hut, a tiny little man with a long, scraggly beard was dancing around a fire, chanting:

'The child is mine.
I've won the game.
Since Rumpelstiltskin
is my name.' "

Now the Queen came to know the dwarf's secret !

"Is your name Sheepshanks or Spindleshanks, Haskell or Horner?" asked the Queen.

"Wrong!" cried the dwarf gleefully.

"Let me try one final guess," said the Queen with a smile. "Could your name be Rumpelstiltskin?"

The dwarf turned purple with rage. He screamed. He yelled. He gnashed his teeth. He stomped his foot with such anger that it sank into the ground.

Rumpelstiltskin remained in that same place, frozen forever in his rage.

Printed at : HARCUS New Delhi 49 8686